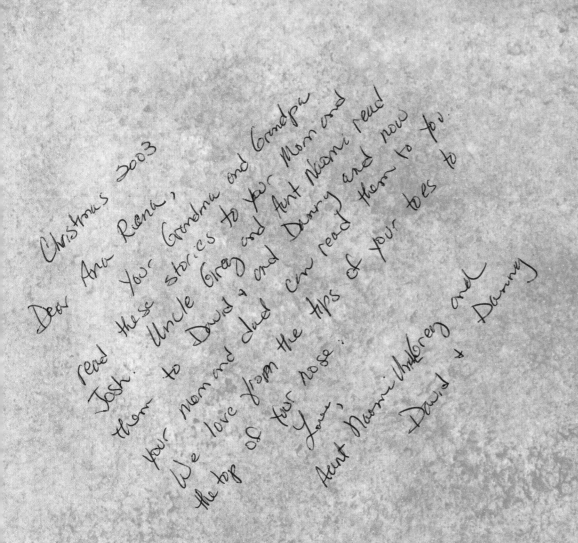

Christmas 2003

Dear Ana Rena,

Your Grandma and Grandpa
read these stories to your Mom and
Josh. Uncle Greg and Aunt Naomi read
them to David and Danny and now
your mom and dad can read them to you.
We love you from the tips of your toes to
the top of your nose.

Love,
Aunt Naomi, Uncle Greg and
David + Danny

KEATS'S NEIGHBORHOOD

AN *EZRA JACK KEATS* TREASURY

KEATS'S NEIGHBORHOOD

With an Introduction by Anita Silvey

VIKING

CONTENTS

INTRODUCTION

As someone who had experienced both poverty and anti-Semitism, Ezra Jack Keats found himself sympathetic to city children from different races and backgrounds who had suffered as he had. These children mattered to him. But in the early 1960s those children's faces, and those experiences, simply did not appear in the books that were published.

Ezra Jack Keats's apprenticeship in children's books began in 1954 and lasted about seven years; in that time he illustrated twenty-five books for other writers, gradually gaining mastery of his craft. Then in 1960 he published *My Dog Is Lost!* Written in collaboration with Pat Cherr, the book featured a Puerto Rican protagonist. In that year Keats also found in his studio a *Life* magazine picture of a small boy from rural Georgia. Intrigued by the boy's face, attitude, and clothing, Keats used him as the model for a young black boy, Peter—the central character of *The*

Snowy Day. On a perfect snowy day, Peter dons his red snowsuit and sets out to explore a magical world.

The Viking editor of *The Snowy Day*, Annis Duff, guided the project with a steady but light hand, making sure that Keats was comfortable with every decision. Duff paid careful attention to each word chosen for the spare text. After seeing the first dummy, she encouraged Keats to create the

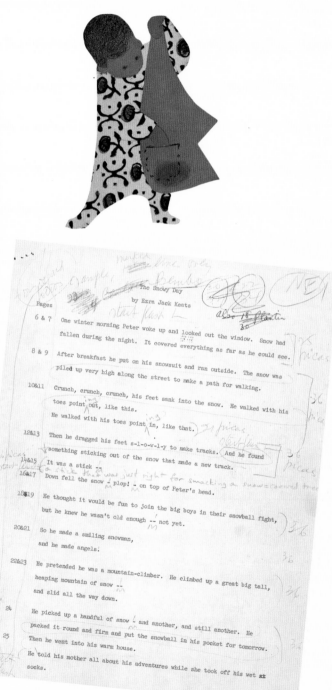

Top left, photo from 1940 *Life* magazine; top, Keats's vision of Peter; bottom, the original manuscript of *The Snowy Day*

entire book in full color—rather than color alternating with black-and-white pages, as had been the original plan. Given the cost of color reproduction at the time and

Top to bottom: the rejected cover sketch for *The Snowy Day* and the original artwork used for the cover of the book.

the difficulties involved in preparing color separations from collage, she obviously knew this decision would be very expensive for Viking. Rejecting Keats's initial sketch for the cover, she argued that "this lovely sympathetic book" needed to feature Peter more prominently on the jacket. Hence the final jacket displays the heartwarming illustration of Peter peering back at his tracks as he walks through the snow. Proudly, Duff presented to the world the first major full-color picture book to portray a black child—often featuring it as the first book in Viking advertisements—although neither the ad copy nor the text of the book ever mentioned Peter's race. So when the book won the Caldecott Award, Annis Duff had every reason to write that she hadn't "been so happy over anything for years."

For *The Snowy Day* and all his other books, Ezra Jack Keats took absolute joy in the creative process, the development of his art, and writing the text to accompany it.

Like so many artists of the postwar period, he turned to the medium of collage because of the freedom and vitality it provided. In the earliest books about Peter, Keats worked in blocks of color, using collage scraps to augment the design. Keats found a piece of Belgian canvas to represent bed linen and spattered india ink on it with a toothbrush to produce a backdrop for Peter's bed. Because the artwork is so spontaneous and ambiguous, the simple images engender stories of their own. Many readers interpret the white space below Peter's sleeping face toward the end of the book as the snowball he created that magical day.

Detail from *The Snowy Day*

In *Jennie's Hat*, Keats brought his pure-collage style to its pinnacle. Jennie's millinery masterpiece incorporates lacy valentines, marbleized papers, postcards, wallpaper, and dried leaves. As his style evolved, Keats turned to a combination of collage and gouache, an opaque watercolor mixed with gum that gives an oil-like glaze.

Detail from *Jennie's Hat*

The typeface proved the only consistent design element in all the books; all were set in his favorite type, Bembo.

The stories in Keats's books always reflected his own personal landscape. An artist lived in apartment 3 of Keats's childhood apartment building. *Goggles!* re-counts the terror Keats experienced from neighborhood bullies. His brother Willie gave his name to Peter's loyal dog companion. Barney in *Louie's Search* was based on a tzaddik, or holy man, whom Keats encountered as a child. Like Peter in *Peter's Chair,* Keats himself once ran away from home, very briefly.

Using these personal memories, Ezra Jack Keats fashioned simple stories that reflected the universal concerns of children: the joys and sorrows of a snowy day, inviting friends to a birthday party, participating in the local pet show, the problems created by a new sibling. In his books these universal experiences are played out in a city environment, with graffiti and peeling paint, dark corners and alleys, a landscape made beautiful by his own vision.

Ezra Jack Keats focused on children's concerns because he cherished his young readers. He often quoted a line from a child's letter: "We like you because you have the mind of a child." His editor for many years, Susan

Sketch from *Goggles!*

Hirschman, remembers how he agonized over mistakes in some of his early books. In one unfortunate drawing for Millicent Selsam's *How Animals Sleep*, he created a guinea pig with a rodent's tail. The error sailed by editors, copy editors, and reviewers, but it did not escape the notice of one particular child, who was distraught because her own guinea pig didn't have such a tail. Keats wrote profoundly apologetic letters to both mother and child, but he never forgot the incident. He was careful after that to get everything in his books as correct as possible.

Even with his attention to detail, he had a rough time with adult critics. As Keats once wistfully wrote, it wasn't all "beer and skittles" for him after he won the Caldecott Medal in 1963. It is often difficult to understand the passion and controversies that many of our classic children's titles raised when they were first published. We laugh now when we hear that attempts were made to ban Munro Leaf's *The Story of Ferdinand*, the tale of a Spanish bull who prefers eating daisies to fighting. Because the book appeared at the time of the Spanish Civil War, Ferdinand's pacifism was seen as a threat by supporters of the war.

To our modern eyes, *The Snowy Day*, a gentle, perfect story of a boy's love of snow, hardly seems as if it could engender heated debates. Yet critics virulently attacked Keats and his books. The opening salvo came in Nancy Larrick's essay "The All White World of Children's Books," which appeared in 1965 in *Saturday*

Review. A well-respected critic and past president of the International Reading Association, Larrick thoroughly castigated the publishing community for the lack of books featuring African-American children. Although she stated that *The Snowy Day* "gives a sympathetic picture of just one child, a small Negro boy," she found the mother a stereotype, "a huge figure in a gaudy yellow plain dress." But the attacks against Keats became more pointed. At the end of the 1960s and during the 1970s, he faced the ire of the Council for Interracial

Detail from *The Snowy Day*

Sketch from *A Letter to Amy*

Books for Children. They claimed that as a white man Keats had no right to fashion books about black characters; in doing so he was stealing money from legitimate African-American creators. Absolutely devastated by the criticism, Keats stopped working altogether. Eventually, his friend Augusta Baker—Coordinator of Children's Services at the New York Public Library and an African-American herself—convinced Keats to put these comments behind him and move on. In the mid 1970s he attempted to answer critics with an article in *The Horn Book Magazine*. Basically humane and caring, he remained deeply wounded for years by all the personal and professional criticism leveled against him.

In choosing to place that black

Detail from *Pet Show!*

face against the white snow, Keats altered children's books forever. Like Nancy Larrick and the Council for Interracial Books for Children, he simply wanted to see children of different races represented in books. The very success of *The Snowy Day* opened the door for other creative individuals. Those publishing books, working with children, and writing books realized that an audience existed that eagerly sought their own faces and lives reflected in their books. Subsequently, the children's book community became enriched by an extraordinarily talented group of African-American authors and illustrators who began their work in the 1960s and 1970s. And if the next generation of African-American creators, their offspring both literally and figuratively—Brian Collier, Brian Pinkney, Chris Myers, Javaka Steptoe—can see farther and have even greater vision, it is because they stand on the shoulders of giants. And one of those giants was named Ezra Jack Keats.

With nearly two million copies in print, *The Snowy Day* alone would confirm Keats's place in the pantheon of great children's book creators. To have made one of the two picture-book masterpieces of the early 1960s (the other being Maurice Sendak's *Where the Wild Things Are*) would be enough of a legacy. But by bringing multicultural publishing to the forefront of our consciousness, Keats has influenced children's books for four decades. Hence his achievements proved even greater than his books.

On the fortieth anniversary of *The Snowy Day,* children and adults alike can celebrate this giant, Ezra Jack Keats, and his accomplishments. Because he could think with the mind of a child, children love his books. Because he remained true to his convictions, adults admire his artistic integrity. With great courage and in the face of adversity, Keats took the less-traveled, more difficult road—and that has made all the difference in children's books.

Anita Silvey
Westwood, Massachusetts
March 8, 2002

THE SNOWY DAY

1962

One winter morning Peter woke up and looked out the window. Snow had fallen during the night. It covered everything as far as he could see.

After breakfast he put on his snowsuit and ran outside. The snow was piled up very high along the street to make a path for walking.

Crunch, crunch, crunch, his feet sank into the snow.
He walked with his toes pointing out, like this:

He walked with his toes
pointing in, like that:

17

Then he dragged his feet s-l-o-w-l-y to make tracks.
And he found something sticking out of the snow that made a new track.

It was a stick—a stick that was just right for smacking a snow-covered tree.

Down fell the snow—plop!—on top of Peter's head.

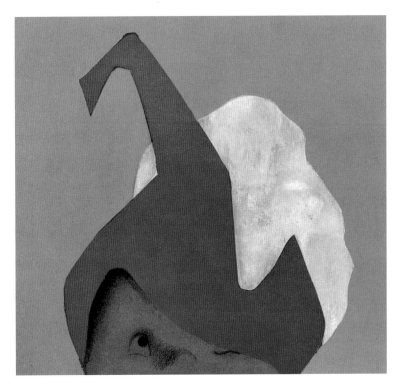

He thought it would be fun to join
the big boys in their snowball fight, but
he knew he wasn't old enough—not yet.

So he made a smiling snowman, and
he made angels.

He pretended he was a mountain-
climber.

He climbed up a great big tall
heaping mountain of snow—and slid
all the way down.

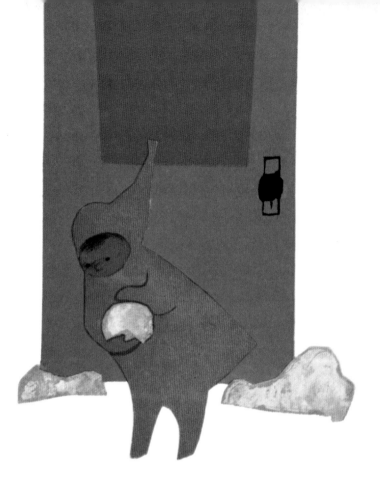

He picked up a handful of snow—and another, and still another. He packed it round and firm and put the snowball in his pocket for tomorrow. Then he went into his warm house.

He told his mother all about his adventures while she took off his wet socks.

And he thought and thought and thought about them.

Before he got into bed he looked in his pocket.

His pocket was empty. The snowball wasn't there.

He felt very sad.

While he slept, he dreamed that the sun had melted all the snow away.

But when he woke up his dream was gone. The snow was still everywhere.

New snow was falling!

After breakfast he called to his friend
from across the hall, and they went out
together into the deep, deep snow.

Original artwork from *John Henry* by Julius Lester and Jerry Pinkney

Detail from *John Henry: An American Legend*, by Ezra Jack Keats

A Word from JERRY PINKNEY

Jerry Pinkney is the award-winning illustrator of numerous books for young readers, many of which celebrate multicultural and African-American themes. He is a four-time recipient of the Caldecott Honor Medal, for *The Ugly Duckling, John Henry, The Talking Eggs,* and *Mirandy and Brother Wind.* He has also received the Coretta Scott King Illustrator Award four times and the honor award five times. He lives with his wife in Westchester County, New York

IN 1983, I received a call from the California African-American Museum inviting me to co-curate an exhibition entitled *Lasting Impressions: Illustrating African-American Children's Books.* The thinking was to include those illustrators whose work demonstrated excellence in portraying people of color. It was important that the works endow the characters with a sense of dignity and self respect, and above all else, that they celebrate African-American life and culture.

Ezra Jack Keats was one of the illustrators who led the list. His role in giving an African-American a central part in the story was a benchmark in mainstream publishing. Using his skill as a painter and his compassion as a humanist, he enthralled, entertained, and educated children as well as adults.

Did Ezra think of himself as courageous for presenting realistic images of black families? Was he an advocate for the disenfranchised, for those who were left out of the mainstream? I suspect he simply saw all people with heart, eyes, and paintbrush equally. He enlarged the world of children's literature, by instilling his characters with energy and by filling each page with exquisite design and dazzling color.

When Ezra's original art came in, I was struck by how arresting the images are; colors more brilliant and surfaces more compelling than the printed process could possibly duplicate.

At that time, I had begun the illustration work for *John Henry,* a book I had written in collaboration with Julius Lester. For inspiration I turned to Ezra Jack Keats's *John Henry: An American Legend,* and my task was made less daunting.

WHISTLE FOR WILLIE

1964

Oh, how Peter wished he could whistle!

He saw a boy playing with his dog. Whenever the boy whistled, the dog ran straight to him.

Peter tried and tried to whistle, but he couldn't.

So instead he began to turn himself around—around and around he whirled . . . faster and faster. . . .

When he stopped everything turned down . . .

and up . . .

and up . . .

and down . . .

and around

and around.

Peter saw his dog, Willie, coming.

Quick as a wink, he hid in an empty carton lying on the sidewalk.

"Wouldn't it be funny if I whistled?" Peter thought.

"Willie would stop and look all around to see who it was."

Peter tried again to whistle—but still he couldn't.

So Willie just walked on.

Peter got out of the carton and
started home.

On the way he took some colored
chalks out of his pocket and drew a
long, long line right up to his door.

He stood there and tried to whistle
again.

He blew till his cheeks were tired.

But nothing happened.

He went into his house and put on his father's old hat to make himself feel more grown-up.

He looked into the mirror to practice whistling.

Still no whistle!

When his mother saw what he was doing, Peter pretended that he was his father.

He said, "I've come home early today, dear. Is Peter here?"

His mother answered, "Why no, he's outside with Willie."

"Well, I'll go out and look for them," said Peter.

First he walked along a crack in the sidewalk.

Then he tried to run away from his shadow.

He jumped off his shadow. But when he landed they were together again.

He came to the corner where the carton was, and who should he see but Willie!

Peter scrambled under the carton. He blew and blew and blew. Suddenly— out came a real whistle!

Willie stopped and looked around to see who it was.

"It's me," Peter shouted, and stood up. Willie raced straight to him.

Peter ran home to show his father and mother what he could do. They loved Peter's whistling. So did Willie.

Peter's mother asked him and Willie to go on an errand to the grocery store.
He whistled all the way there, and he whistled all the way home.

A
LETTER
TO AMY

1968

"I'm writing a letter to Amy. I'm inviting her to my party," Peter announced.

"Why don't you just ask her? You didn't write to anyone else," said his mother.

Peter stared at the sheet of paper for a while and said, "We-e-el-l, this way it's sort of special."

He folded the letter quite a few times, put it in the envelope, and sealed it.

"Now I'll mail it," he said.

"What did you write?" his mother asked.

WILL YOU PLEASE
COME TO MY BIRTHDAY
PARTY. PETER.

"You should tell her when to come."
So he wrote on the back of the envelope: IT IS THIS SATURDAY AT 2.

"Now I'll mail it."

"Put on a stamp."

He did, and started to leave.

"Wear your raincoat. It looks like rain."

He put it on and said, "It looks like rain. You'd better stay in, Willie," and ran out to mail his letter.

Walking to the mailbox, Peter looked at the sky.

Dark clouds raced across it like wild horses.

He glanced up at Amy's window. She wasn't there. Only Pepe, her parrot, sat peering down.

"Willie! Didn't I tell you to stay home?"

Peter thought, What will the boys say when they see a girl at my party?

Suddenly there was a flash of lightning and a roar of thunder!

A strong wind blew the letter out of his hand!

Peter chased the letter.

He tried to stop it with his foot, but it blew away.

Then it flew high into the air—and landed, skipping across a hopscotch game.

The letter blew this way and that.
Peter chased it this way and that.

He couldn't catch it.

Big drops of rain began to fall.

Just then someone turned the corner.

It was Amy! She waved to him. The letter flew right toward her.

She mustn't see it, or the surprise will be spoiled!

They both ran for the letter.

In his great hurry, Peter bumped into Amy.

He caught the letter before she could see it was for her.

Quickly he stuffed the letter into the mailbox.

He looked for Amy, but she had run off crying.

Now she'll never come to my party,
thought Peter.
He saw his reflection in the street.
It looked all mixed up.

When Peter got back to his house, his mother asked, "Did you mail your letter?"

"Yes," he said sadly.

Saturday came at last.

Everybody arrived but Amy.

"Shall I bring the cake out now?" his mother asked Peter.

"Let's wait a little," said Peter.

"Now! Bring it out now!" chanted the boys.

"All right," said Peter slowly, "bring it out now."

Just then the door opened.
In walked Amy with her parrot!
"A girl—ugh!" said Eddie.

"Happy Birthday, Peter!" said Amy.
"HAAPPY BIRRRTHDAY,
PEEETERRR!" repeated the parrot.

Peter's mother brought in the cake
she had baked and lit the candles.
Everyone sang.

"Make a wish!" cried Amy.

"Wish for a truck full of ice cream!"
shouted Eddie.

"A store full of candy and no
stomach-ache!"

But Peter made his own wish,
and blew out all the candles at once.

PETER'S CHAIR

1967

Peter stretched as high as he could.
There! His tall building was finished.

CRASH! Down it came.
"Shhhh!" called his mother.
"You'll have to play more quietly.
Remember, we have a new baby in
the house."

Peter looked into his sister Susie's room.

His mother was fussing around the cradle.

"That's my cradle," he thought, "and they painted it pink!"

"Hi, Peter," said his father.

"Would you like to help paint sister's high chair?"

"It's my high chair," whispered Peter.

He saw his crib and muttered, "My crib. It's painted pink too."

Not far away stood his old chair.

"They didn't paint that yet!" Peter shouted.

He picked it up and ran to his room.

"Let's run away, Willie," he said.

Peter filled a shopping bag with cookies and dog biscuits.

"We'll take my blue chair, my toy crocodile, and the picture of me when I was a baby."

Willie got his bone.

They went outside and stood in front of his house.

"This is a good place," said Peter.

He arranged his things very nicely and decided to sit in his chair for a while.

But he couldn't fit in the chair. He was too big!

His mother came to the window and called, "Won't you come back to us, Peter dear? We have something very special for lunch."

Peter and Willie made believe they didn't hear. But Peter got an idea.

Soon his mother saw signs that
Peter was home.
"That rascal is hiding behind the
curtain," she said happily.

She moved the curtain away.
But he wasn't there!
"Here I am," shouted Peter.

Peter sat in a grown-up chair.
His father sat next to him.
"Daddy," said Peter, "let's paint
the little chair pink for Susie."

And they did.

57

Original artwork from *Joseph Had a Little Overcoat*, by Simms Taback

Detail from *Over in the Meadow*, by Ezra Jack Keats

A Word from SIMMS TABACK

Photo by Marion Goldman

Simms Taback has illustrated many children's books, including *There Was an Old Lady Who Swallowed a Fly*, a Caldecott Honor Book, and *Joseph Had a Little Overcoat*, which won the Caldecott Medal. He lives in Westchester, New York.

I FIRST MET Ezra Jack Keats in the early 1960s when I rented studio space in a building in which he worked and lived (appropriately enough, the building was named The Picasso). I had just started illustrating my first children's book, and Ezra was working on his artwork for *The Snowy Day*.

When I visited Ezra in his studio one day, there were sheets of paper on which he had applied and freely splattered paint, tacked up on all his walls, waiting to dry. Was Ezra, the children's book illustrator I knew, really an abstract painter? No. These sheets—in combinations of reds, browns, greens, etc.—were to be cut up in different shapes and used for collage in his illustrations.

How refreshing and exciting it was for me to see how Ezra was working! Though I was limited in how much I could experiment in my advertising assignments, I realized that I, too, could be more playful, and so I introduced collage elements in my work for Children's Television Network, *Sesame Street* magazine, and assignments I was doing for Scholastic. Sometimes, when I was up against a tight deadline, I would execute the artwork entirely in cut paper. It was faster.

Ezra's style is much more representational than mine. But I was enlightened and encouraged by what he did. And I did have him in my mind when I was working on *There Was an Old Lady Who Swallowed a Fly* and later on *Joseph Had a Little Overcoat*. I wasn't thinking only of his technique, which is instantly recognizable, but also of how straightforward, warm, and child-friendly his pictures are.

GOGGLES!

1969

"Archie, look what I found," Peter shouted through the pipe.

"Motorcycle goggles!"

Archie watched Peter through the hole.

He listened and smiled.

Peter ran to the hideout and put on the goggles.

"Aren't they great?" he asked.

Archie smiled and nodded.

Peter said, "Let's go over to your house and sit on the steps."

Archie nodded.

They started off.

Suddenly some big boys appeared.

"Give us those goggles, kid!"

"No, they're mine," Peter said.

His dog Willie growled.

"Archie, hold Willie," said Peter.

Peter stuffed the goggles into his pocket and put up his fists.

Archie gasped.

Peter turned to see if something was wrong.

The next thing he knew he was knocked to the ground.

Everyone stared at the goggles.

Before anyone could move, Willie snatched the goggles and ran through a hole in the fence.

The big boys chased after him.

"Meet you at the hideout," whispered Peter.

"You go this way, I'll go that way. They won't know where we're going. Willie will find us!"

Peter raced to the hideout.

He sank down as low as he could.
Footsteps!

"The big boys! They followed me."
Peter held his breath.

ARCHIE!

What was that?

Archie looked through the hole.

There were the big boys—and there was Willie.

They would see him!

Archie stared at the pipe.

Suddenly he spoke.

"Here, Willie, through the pipe—fast!"

WILLIE!

Peter peeked through
the hole.
The big boys
were coming—
closer and
closer.

Peter took a deep breath.

Then he yelled through the pipe, "Willie—meet us at the parking lot!"

"Head for the parking lot!" one of the big boys yelled. "Let's go!"

Peter, Archie and Willie crept out of the hideout.

When they reached the fence they got up and ran.

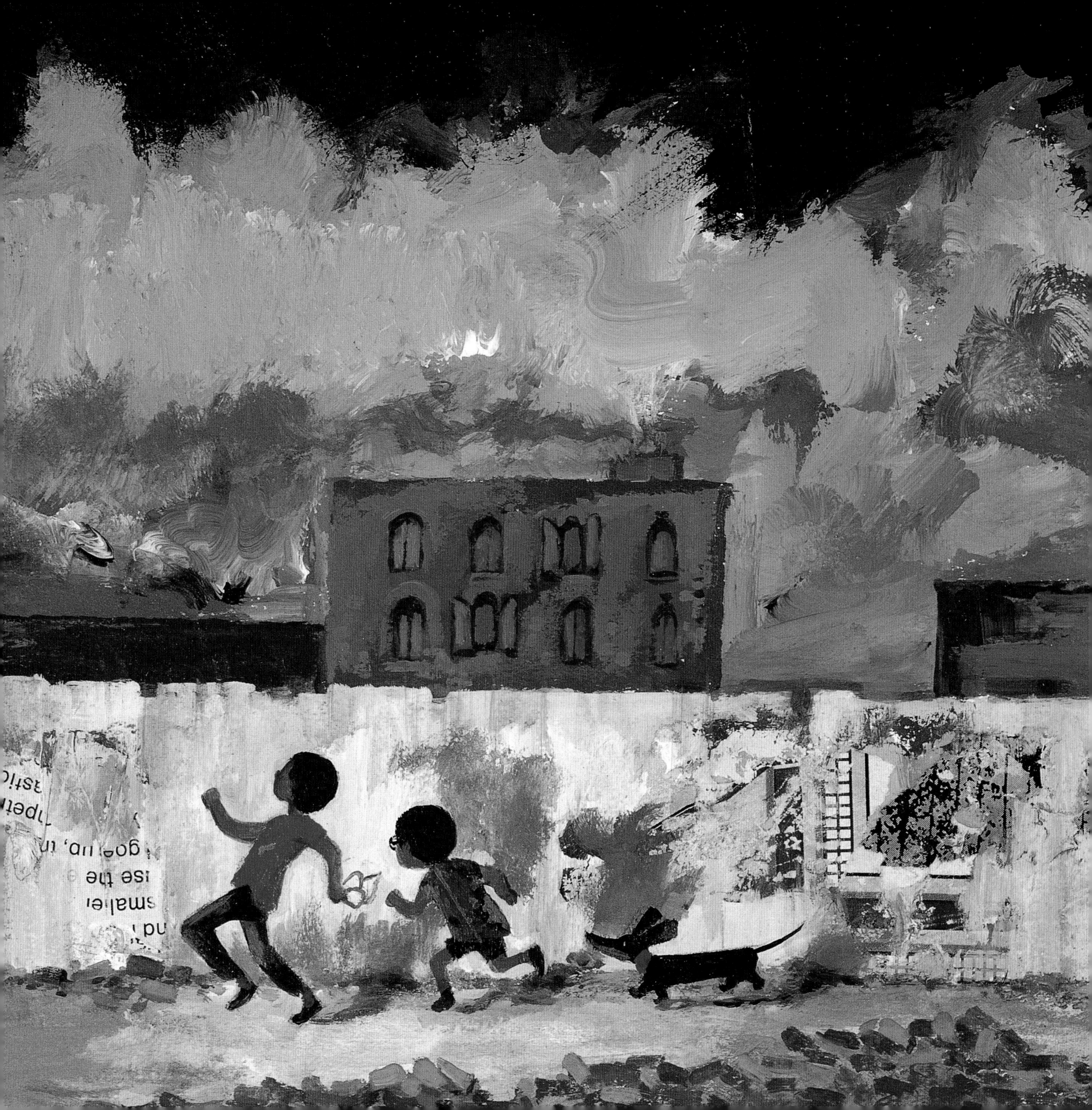

They got to Archie's house.

Archie laughed and said, "We sure fooled 'em, didn't we?"

"We sure did," said Peter, handing him the goggles.

"Things look real fine now," Archie said.

"They sure do," said Peter.

JENNIE'S
HAT

1966

A new hat!

Jennie's favorite aunt promised to send her one as a present.

Jennie waited, and dreamed, and waited.

Shutting her eyes, she sighed, "It'll be big, and flowery, and oh—so very beautiful."

At last it came.

She ran to her room and opened the box.

"Oh, no!" she gasped.

"It's such a *plain* hat!"

"Why, dear, I really think it's quite nice," her mother said kindly.

Jennie blinked back her tears and put the hat under her bed.

She put on a straw basket to see what sort of hat it would make.

Then she drew pictures.

"HAT-CHOO!" she sneezed.

"Bless you, dear," called her mother, "and what are you doing?"

"I'm drawing a hat-erpillar—I mean a caterpillar," answered Jennie.

"Oh, dear," sighed her mother. "I see."

Then she tried on a lampshade, and a little flower pot, a TV antenna, and a shiny pan.

But none of these would do, not really!

Jennie noticed that it was three o'clock.

Time to feed the birds!

She ran to the cupboard, filled a paper bag with bread crumbs, and started for the park.

The birds expected her, for every Saturday afternoon she went to the very same spot to scatter crumbs.

And birds came!

All sorts of birds, fluttering and twittering and cooing.

They all knew Jennie.

Some ate out of her hand.

Others hopped happily on her head.

Soon every last crumb was gone, and away they flew!

For a while Jennie forgot about her new hat.

But walking home, Jennie remembered, and wished out loud. "Oh, I wish my new hat were just a little fancier."

The next morning Jennie got up
early and peeped out the window.
What lovely hats she saw!

Later, she went to church with her father, mother, and friends.
All around her hats appeared like flowers in a garden.

As they left the church Jennie saw some birds . . . then more and more birds.

Were they following her?

They fluttered down to her plain hat, carrying red and violet flowers, and leaves, colored eggs, and a paper fan.

They added a picture of swans on a quiet lake and some big red and yellow roses.

And two big green and orange leaves, more pictures, and some paper flowers, more real flowers, and a pink valentine.

Then all the birds swooped down together, flapping and fluttering around Jennie's new hat.

Suddenly they all flew away.

On Jennie's head sat the *most* beautiful hat.

At the very top was a nest of chirping young birds!

Jennie felt like chirping too.

Happy from head to toe, she felt she was walking on air.

People stared in wonder.

Behind her flew the birds, watchful and proud.

When they all reached her house, the birds, twittering and singing, picked up the nest of little ones and flew back to their home in the park.

Jennie waved good-bye.

"Thank you!" she called.

Jennie's mother helped her wrap the wonderful hat, piled high with lovely things. Even after the flowers and leaves had dried, it would be saved and looked at and remembered for a long, long time.

HI, CAT!

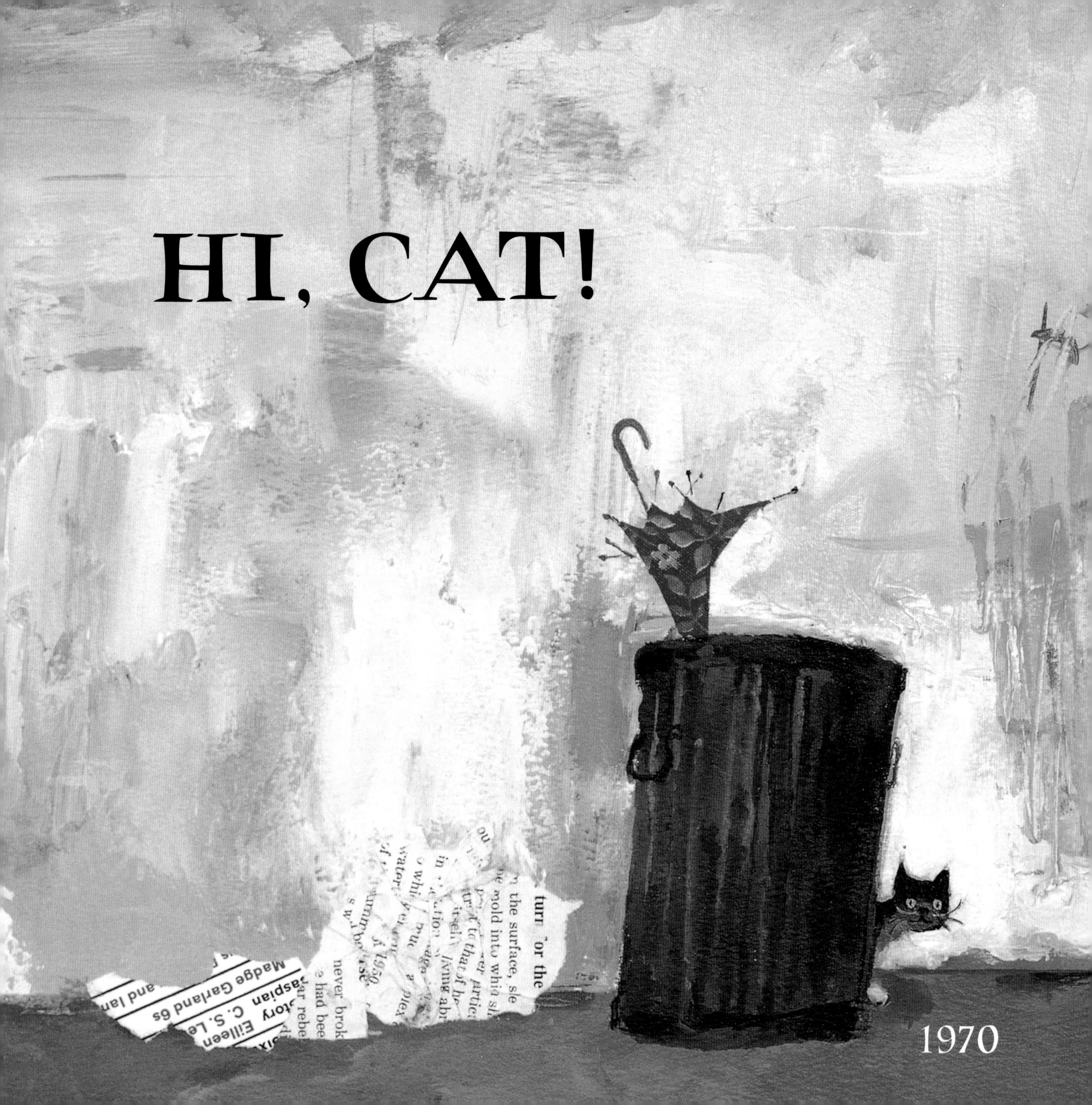

1970

On his way to meet Peter, Archie saw someone new on the block.

"Hi, cat," he said as he walked by.

He looked at his reflection in a store window.

Peter was waiting at the corner.

"Make way for your ol' gran'pa,"
Archie said in a shaky voice.

He looked Peter up and down.

"My, my, Peter, how you've grown!"

"Why, gran'pa," Peter
said. "It's good to see you."

"Hello, my children," Archie
croaked.

"Hi, gran'pa!" Susy giggled.

Willie was so happy to see
Archie he ran over and licked his face.
Archie tasted delicious!
Willie licked and licked and licked.
"No respect for old age!"

Archie whispered
something to Peter and
ran off.
"Stick around,
folks," Peter called.
"We have a
surprise for you."

When Archie got back, he and
Peter worked while everyone waited.

"OK!" Peter announced. "Make way for
Mister Big Face!"
A big paper bag appeared.
Then a tongue stuck out of one of the eyes!

A hand came out of an ear and motioned everyone to move closer. They all obeyed.

Suddenly the bag began to shake.

It shook harder, and harder, and—

MEEOOW!

People started to leave.

"Wait—wait—the show'll go on!
See the tallest dog in the world take
a walk!" Archie shouted.

"Some show, gran'pa!"

"Some tall dog!"

"Who ate your mustache, gran'pa?"

Everyone walked away, laughing.

Soon no one was left except

Archie, Peter, Willie and the torn

paper bag.

"It would have been great if it wasn't for that crazy cat," said Peter as they walked home.

"Mmmm," said Archie. "He sure stuck around."

"...and all I said was 'Hi, cat,'" said Archie, finishing his story.

"You're well rid of a cat like that," said his mother.

Archie thought for a while.

"You know what, Ma?" he said. "I think that cat just kinda liked me!"

Original artwork from *Running the Road to ABC*, by Denize Lauture and Reynold Ruffins

A Word from REYNOLD RUFFINS

Reynold Ruffins has designed and illustrated many distinguished children's books. Some of his previous books include *Running the Road to ABC*, for which he won a Coretta Scott King Illustrator Award, and *Misoso*. He and his wife live in Sag Harbor, New York.

Original artwork from *The King's Fountain*, by Lloyd Alexander and Ezra Jack Keats

OK, GET THIS. There was this guy with a whispery, gravelly voice and a craggy prospector's face. His mustache was styled somewhere between Pecos Bill and an Oxford don. His name . . . Keats, Ezra Jack Keats. And what did he do? He turned snow into gold.

As a young illustrator, I was more interested in the bigger bucks and fast turnaround of the advertising business. So I was a bit bewildered by Ezra's great dedication to kids' books. He could spend days considering character, color, and composition. I've watched him ponder one or another color of paper he had hand dipped, trying to choose between them. All such decisions were painstakingly arrived at. Yet from this effort, he panned a golden classic—*The Snowy Day*.

Ezra was the older, wiser, more serious practitioner of the craft. It was not until *I* began, years later, to illustrate children's books that I could fully appreciate the true value of his efforts and how our association influenced the way I approached my work.

Reading *The Snowy Day* to our children was extra special; not only was it the work of a friend, it was also the very first time the central figure was their color. In the sixties Ezra believed there should be children's book characters other than Dick and Jane, their Granny, and her damn blue birds. And he did something about it.

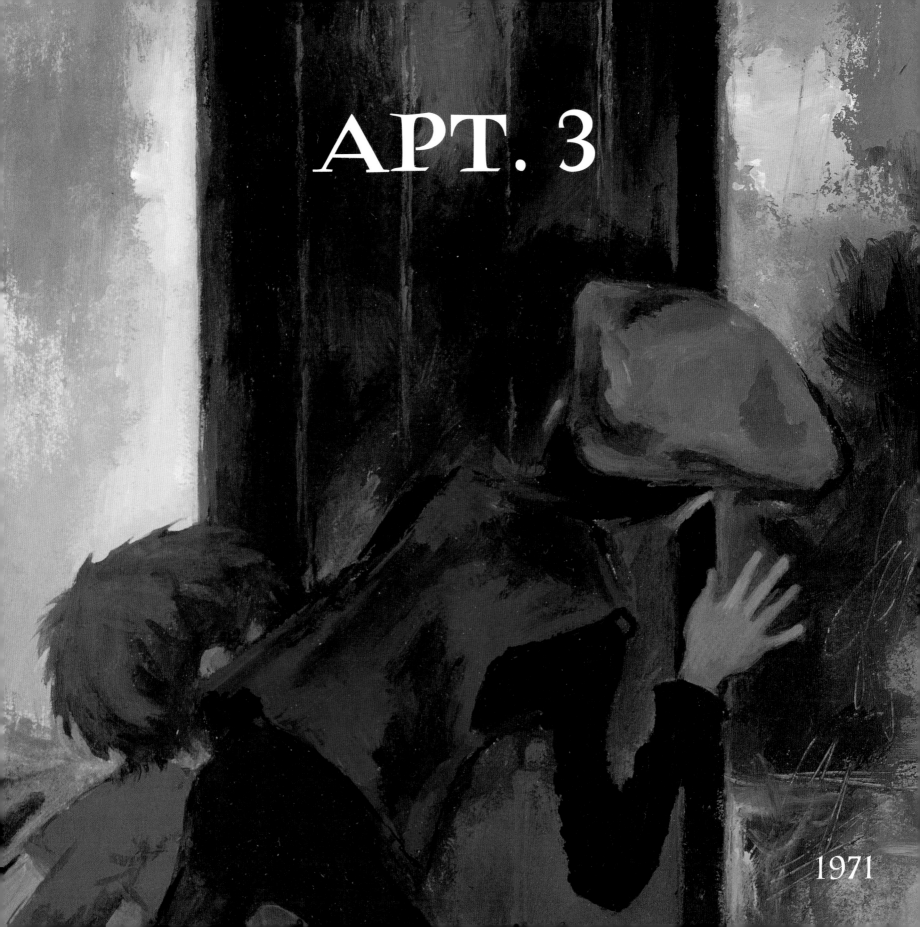

APT. 3

1971

The rain fell steadily.

It beat against the windows, softening the sounds of the city.

As Sam gazed out, he heard someone in the building playing a harmonica.

It filled him with sad and lonely feelings—like the rain outside.

He had heard that music before.

Each time it was different.

"Who's that playing?" Sam wondered.

Sam went into the hall and listened. No music.
His little brother Ben tagged along.
Sam listened at the door across the hall.
Crunch, crunch, crunch.
Crunch, crackle, crunch!
Someone—or something—turned the knob.

Out came Mr. Muntz, crunching
a mouthful of potato chips.

They waited until he was gone.

There was one door left on their
floor.

Through it came smells of cigarettes
and cooking.

A family was arguing.

But no music.

They walked down to the floor below.

A dog was barking—real mean—in Apt. 9.

Next door a mother sang softly to her crying baby.

At Apt. 7, not a sound.

Down another flight.

The hall light was broken.

At Apt. 6, there was a ball game on TV. It sounded like a million people were in there cheering.

Apt. 5—loud, juicy snoring.

Ben bumped into an old, worn-out mattress.

"That snorer sure's enjoying his new one," Sam said.

Apt. 4—more yelling.

Finally, the ground floor.

The door of Apt. 1 opened.

"The super!" Sam whispered.

They hid under the stairs.

The super grumbled to himself as he left the building and slammed the door.

"That guy hates everyone," said Ben.

Apt. 3 was quiet.

Just a container of milk outside the door.

They stopped in front of Apt. 2—Betsy's door.

Sam thought, "Maybe she'll come out and I'll say hello to her."

He decided to hang around.

"Let's rest a little," he said.

They sat on the steps.

But no Betsy.

And no music.

"C'mon, let's go home," said Ben.

As they turned to go upstairs, Sam noticed that the container of milk was gone!

He went over to take a good look.
The door was open a little.
He peeked in.
"WELL?" A sharp voice startled Sam.
"We didn't take the milk!" he blurted.
But the man was shouting, "O.K., nosy! Have a good look!"
Sam could make out a figure at a table.
It was the blind man's apartment!
"Come on in, you two! What's the matter—scared?"

They were so scared they went in.

"There's the milk," Sam shouted. "We didn't take it!"

"Who said you did?" snapped the man. "I brought it in myself. Stop shaking, kids. Shut the door and sit down."

Sam shut the door and sat down.

"How'd you know we're kids?" asked Ben.

"I know about you boys. You live upstairs," said the man. "I know something else about you, Sam."

"What?" whispered Sam.

"You like the little girl across the hall.

The way you slow down when you pass her door. The real nice way you say 'Hi, Betsy,' and she says 'Hi, Sam.'"

Ben giggled.

Sam jumped up.

"Who's nosy now?" he yelled. "I know about you too. You sit around here, finding out other people's secrets!"

The man's face took on a faraway look.

"I know plenty, young fellow. I know when it rains, when it snows, what people are cooking, and what they think they're fighting about. Secrets? You want to hear some secrets? Listen."

He stood up suddenly, raised his harmonica to his mouth, and began to play.

He played purples and grays and rain and smoke and the sounds of night.

Sam sat quietly and listened.

He felt that all the sights and sounds and colors from outside had come into the room and were floating around.

He floated with them.

Ben's eyes were closed, and he was smiling.

After a while, Sam turned to the man and said, "Would you like to take a walk with us tomorrow?"

The music became so soft and quiet they could barely hear it.

Then the dark room filled with wild, noisy, happy music.

It bounced from wall to wall.

Sam and Ben looked at each other.

They couldn't wait for tomorrow.

Detail from *The Very Hungry Caterpillar*, by Eric Carle

A Word from ERIC CARLE

Eric Carle is the popular creator of many books for young children, including the celebrated classic *The Very Hungry Caterpillar.* His artwork is created with collage technique, using hand-painted papers which he cuts and layers to form bright and cheerful images. He lives with his wife in Northampton, Massachusetts.

Details from *Over in the Meadow*, by Ezra Jack Keats

IN THE MID sixties, after I had illustrated my first book, *Brown Bear, Brown Bear, What Do You See?* for Bill Martin Jr., a friend offered to introduce me to Ezra Keats, the Caldecott Medal winner.

Ezra who? The Caldecott what? You see, so far I had been a total novice in the field of picture books.

Soon Ezra and I met for lunch. I would say Ezra's sparkling eyes were the first impression I had of this gentle and kind man. After lunch, Ezra invited me to his apartment/studio where he showed me his beautiful marbled papers and demonstrated how he prepared them. As the afternoon stretched on, he told me about publishing, royalties, contracts, editors, and other picture book artists. That day, Ezra opened a new world to me.

I wondered whether it was possible to earn a living illustrating and writing books for children—illustrating *Brown Bear* had been fun, but would it pay the bills?

Yes, replied Ezra. It is possible to earn a living.

From strangers and colleagues we moved on to become friends. Soon we were having dinners together. I remember parties at his or my place, or somewhere in the Village or the Upper East Side. We did not always speak about books; I remember Ezra as having a keen eye for beautiful women!

But most of all, I remember his generous spirit. He was an experienced professional who reached out to me, a greenhorn at the threshold of entering the world of picture book making.

And, oh, I will always remember his sparking eyes.

"What kind of neighborhood is this?" thought Louie.

"Nobody notices a kid around here."

Louie put on some funny things and took a walk.

Maybe someone would notice him—someone he'd like for a father.

Louie passed quite a few people.

He looked them over, and walked on.

People were going up and down, and in and out.

He wanted to say something to them, but they were too busy.

Louie walked backward, still looking at them.

He bumped into a man carrying a big cake.

"Watch where you're going!" the man yelled.

Louie turned around and walked forward.

As he got closer, something fell off. Louie picked it up to put it back. It began to play music!

The man in the truck turned around.

He looked terrible!

"Hey!" he yelled. "What are you doing with that?"

Louie was so scared, he couldn't speak.

He saw a truck piled high with old furniture.

The man jumped off the truck, and chased Louie.

"Come back, you little crook!" he bellowed.

Louie fell!

The man stared down at him.

"You stole it!" he shouted. "Where do you live?"

"No, I didn't steal it," Louie cried. "Ow! Ow! My foot!"

Louie pointed to where he lived.

They went into his house.

"Louie! What happened?" his mother gasped. "And who are you?"

"Your son's a crook!"

"What? IMPOSSIBLE! He's the best boy in the world!"

"Ow! Ow! He broke my foot!" Louie cried.

"Really? You're still standing on it— and what's that music I hear?"

Louie saw that he was still holding the box.

He dropped it.

BANG! It stopped playing.

"Now you broke my beautiful music maker!" the man boomed. "You'll pay for this!"

The house got quiet.

"WELL, WHAT ARE YOU GOING TO DO?" the man shouted, shaking his fists in the air.

The whole room shook. The music box began to play.

The man looked around, surprised.

"Err—ya know what? That thing never played like that for me before," said the man.

"See? And you blamed Louie," his mother said. "If I know him, he was only trying to put it back."

Louie nodded.

"Well—in that case—I'm sorry," the man mumbled.

He picked up the box and started to leave.

Then he turned around and said, "Since it plays so good for you, Louie, why don't you keep it? Here's the windup key."

Louie jumped up and down.

His foot felt fine.

"By the way," said the man, "my name's Barney," and he bowed a little.

"My name's Peg, and, of course, you know my son, Louie."

"Hello," said Louie. "Do you have a boy of your own?"

"Nope. Just me and my business."

"Would you like a cup of tea?" asked Peg.

A few days later Barney returned. He took them in his truck to the waterfront.

Barney knew just about everybody!

The tugboat men gave them a ride on their boat.

Barney visited Louie and Peg again and again.

Then, one Sunday, at the end of summer . . .

Barney and Peg got married!

They had a wonderful wedding.

And all their friends and neighbors came.

PET SHOW!

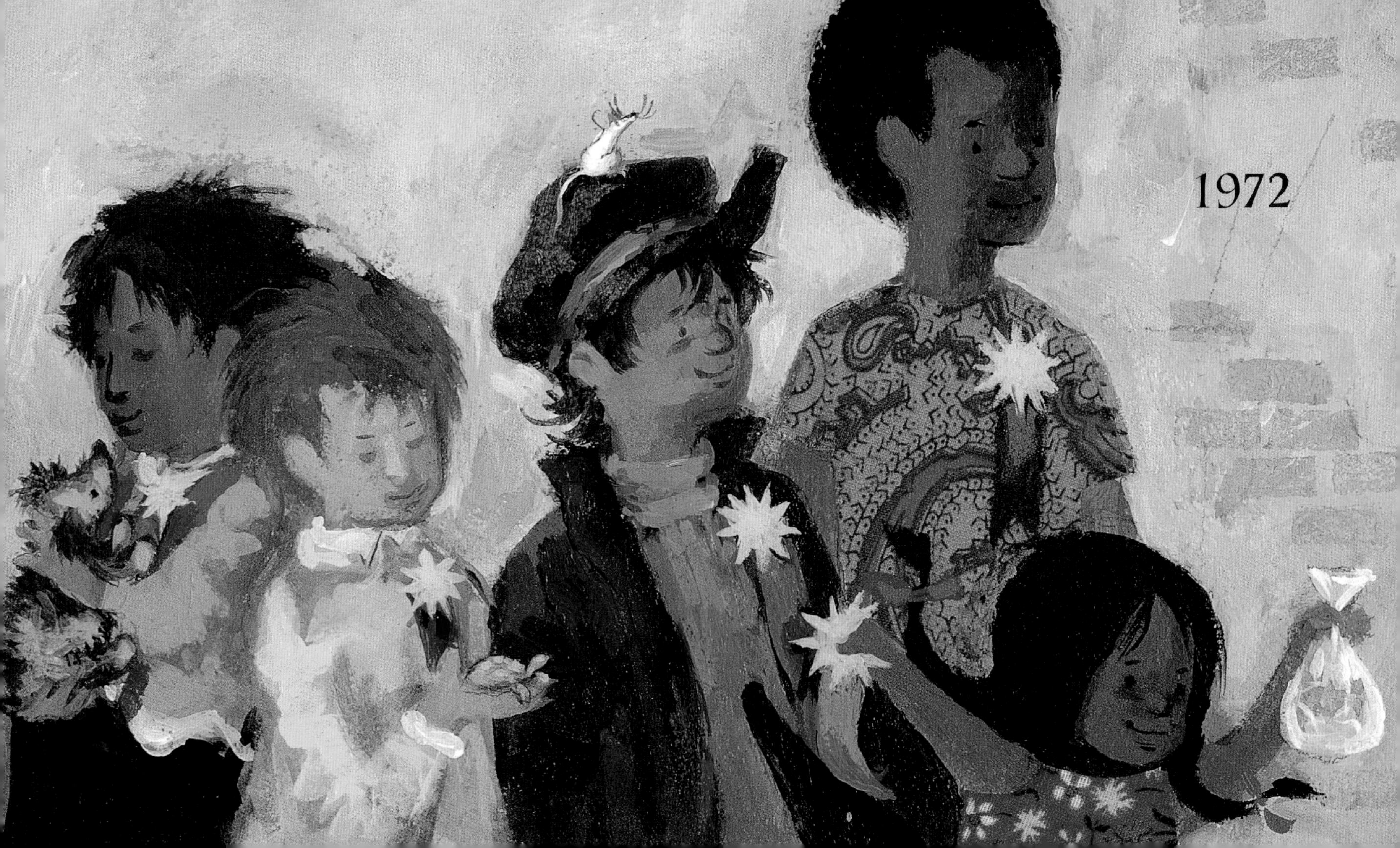

1972

Everyone was talking about the pet show.

The kids told each other about the pets they would bring.

Matt said he would bring ants!

"I'm gonna bring my mouse!" bragged Roberto.

"What are you gonna bring, Archie—the cat?"

"Uh-huh," said Archie.

The next day they all got ready for the
pet show.

"Where's the cat?" Archie called.

"Anyone see the cat?"

Archie and Willie looked in the cat's
favorite hangouts, while Peter and Susie
searched up and down the street.

No cat.

Archie's mother came to
the window.

"Where can that cat be?"
he asked her.

"You know how independent he is, Archie.
You never know when to expect him."

"But I expect him now! It's time for the pet
show! Maybe he's inside somewhere."

Archie ran into the building.

After a while he came to the window.

"I can't find him. I looked all over the place. You'd better start without me."

"Gee, we're sorry, Archie," said Peter.

"So long," said Susie.

They got to the entrance.
A lot of people were already there.
Just then, Roberto's mouse took off.
Willie chased the mouse.

Roberto chased Willie.
Peter chased Roberto.
Susie chased Peter—and the show started.

"Line up with your pets, please!" the judges called.

They walked up and down looking carefully at every pet, and asking, "How old is your pet?" and "What's your pet's name?"

Everyone got a prize for something.

There was the noisiest parrot, the handsomest frog, the friendliest fishes, the yellowest canary, the busiest ants, the brightest goldfish, the longest dog, the fastest mouse, the softest puppy, the slowest turtle—and many more!

As the last prize was being awarded, someone shouted, "Look—here comes Archie!"

"Hello. You're just in time!" a judge said. "What's in that bag?"

"My pet."

"May I see it, please?"

At that moment the cat showed up.

The other judge called out, "A blue ribbon to the nice lady for the cat with the longest whiskers."

Before anyone could say anything, he pinned a blue ribbon on the old woman and came back to Archie.

"What kind of a pet have you got in that jar?"

"A germ!" answered Archie.

"Mmmm—and what's your germ's name?"

Archie thought for a moment. "Al," he said.

The judges whispered to each other. "A blue ribbon for Al, the quietest pet in the show!" the judges announced.

As everyone was leaving, the old woman came over to Archie.

"He's really your cat, isn't he?" she said. "You should have the ribbon."

"It's OK," Archie said. "You keep it." And he ran to join his friends.

They passed the old woman on their way home.

"Thank you for the ribbon," she called. Archie smiled.

"It looks good on you. See you around."

"See you around," she said.

ABOUT THE AUTHOR

Ezra Jack Keats was born Jacob Ezra Katz on March 11, 1916, the third child of Benjamin and Augusta Podgainy Katz, Polish immigrants of Jewish descent. Young Ezra displayed clear artistic abilities from a very early age, which his mother secretly nurtured and his father openly disapproved of, fearing that an artist would never make a good living. Indeed, during the Depression while he was growing up, there was barely enough money to put food on the table or pay rent on the family's crowded tenement apartment—much less buy canvases and paints for Ezra. Nevertheless, Ezra found a way to express what he saw, drawing pictures on whatever material he could lay his hands on—from paper bags to discarded pieces of wood he found in the trash. Even the top of the family's kitchen table was used as a drawing surface.

Ezra attended public school in Brooklyn beginning in 1923, went on to junior high, and graduated from high school in 1935. In the intervening years, he made friends with other children like himself— kids who were interested in art, music, and politics, kids who led equally impoverished lives and longed to change them. These interests and ideals found their way into his work, and in 1934 Ezra was awarded first place in the National Scholastic Art Competition for an oil painting called *Shantytown*, which put a bleak but realistic face on the state of poverty and unemployment. Several local newspapers covered the story. His father, however, still opposed to Ezra's pursuit of fine arts, never acknowledged his son's early success. Ironically, it was Ezra's paintings that had helped the family get by when his father had lost his job at a Manhattan diner some years earlier; Ezra was able to trade his paintings for a reduction on the bill the family owed to their

Top, the young Ezra Jack Keats; above, *Shantytown*

Keats's portrait of his parents

introduced him to well-known painters, and upon graduation he received a scholarship offer to an art school in Manhattan. But pursuing a degree in the fine arts was not to be. Aware of his family's dependence on him for financial support, Ezra took a job instead with the Works Progress Administration, or WPA, and later signed on as a background illustrator for Captain Marvel comics. In 1943, at the age of twenty-seven, he joined the army, with visions of fighting the Nazis.

Above, Keats (at right) at Captain Marvel comics; right, World War II army photo; far right, Bedford Street, New York

Yet even in wartime, Ezra was valued for his artistic skills. He was sent to Tallahassee, Florida, where he designed camouflage patterns for the army. When the war ended two years later, Ezra was discharged as a corporal, with several honorable service medals to his name.

Ezra returned to New York with feelings of restlessness. He had no job prospects and no place to live, and the anti-Semitic sentiment World War II had been fought partly to wipe out proved alive and well—even in America. Job postings went so far as to say "Jews need not apply." Dis-

grocer. Sadly, Benjamin Katz died shortly before Ezra was to graduate from high school. It was only when Ezra was called upon to identify the body that he discovered the pride his father had taken in his paintings; his father's wallet was overflowing with clippings and articles about his son's work.

Despite this lack of outward support from his father, there were others in his life who noticed and encouraged Ezra's talent. Teachers

couraged by such prejudice, Jacob Ezra Katz officially changed his name to the one now known to readers throughout the world: Ezra Jack Keats.

Visiting Paris had been a long-time dream of Keats's, and using grant money from the GI Bill of Rights, he set sail for France in 1949. There he immersed himself in the artistic scene, sketching everything he saw as he walked the city streets, and even managing to sell several paintings not long after his arrival. A trip that had been planned to last just a month or two soon stretched into a year.

For artists like Keats, there was work to be had illustrating magazine covers and advertisements. When he returned to New York and a friend suggested he visit publishing companies, Keats quickly made the rounds, leaving samples of his work with all the major houses. The initial response was not encouraging. But soon a publisher called and offered him a job illustrating a dust jacket, and it wasn't long before other publishers

were lining up with assignments for him. In 1954, Crowell editor Elizabeth Riley was passing the Doubleday Bookstore on Fifth

Right, Keats in Paris; below, color sketch from Paris; bottom, a Paris street scene

Avenue when a window display caught her eye. The display featured artwork that Keats had created for the dust jacket of *The Easter Party*, by Victoria Sackville-West. Riley arranged to meet with Keats, and soon after commissioned him to do his very first work for a children's book, *Jubilant for Sure*, by Elizabeth Lansing. Without realizing it, Keats had at last fallen into a field that celebrated

Pen-and-ink illustration for Keats's first children's book, *Jubilant for Sure*

Cover of *The Easter Party*

the talents and passions he had spent his whole life developing.

Though written with another author, *My Dog Is Lost!* (1960) was Keats's first attempt to tell a story and illustrate it himself, according to his own vision. The urban neighborhood and multicultural characters he depicts hint at a world relatively unknown in mainstream children's publishing—but very well known to him. It was the kind of neighborhood he had grown up in, and *My Dog Is Lost!* set the stage for the book that would literally change the face of children's books and earn Keats a place in publishing history.

Detail from *My Dog Is Lost!*

Throughout his life, Keats had accumulated a vast amount of reference materials, including photos, images, and magazine clippings. When he embarked on the journey to both write and illustrate a picture book for children entirely by himself, it was the face of a young black boy that spoke to him from the bulletin board where his photo had been tacked. Keats decided it was time to give black children a character who looked like them, and who spoke to them and to their experiences. And he knew without a doubt that this boy, whom he called Peter, would be the hero of that book, *The Snowy Day*.

The use of an African-American central character was not the only ground-breaking decision that went into the creation of *The Snowy Day*. In a departure from his other books, Keats chose collage as his medium, layering cut or torn pieces of fabrics and papers with his paintings to arrive at patterns and expressive images that had never before been seen. The book was published in 1962, and in 1963 was awarded the most prestigious

Detail of color study for *Peter's Chair*

prize in picture book illustration, the Caldecott Medal.

Peter appeared in several more picture books, including *Whistle for Willie, Goggles!* (a Caldecott Honor book), *Peter's Chair, A Letter to Amy, Pet Show*, and *Hi, Cat!*. However, the characters and plots of many of Keats's books can be traced to his own childhood: Peter's beloved dog, Willie, is named for Keats's older brother, while the blind man in *Apt. 3* was once a downstairs neighbor of the Keats family. Keats himself even makes appearances in some of his books, including *Pet Show!* and *Louie's Search*.

Left, young model posing as the character Sam for *Apt. 3*; below, pencil sketch of Sam for *Apt. 3*

Pencil sketch for the cover of *Hi, Cat!* (note the original title, *A Cat Like That*)

Pencil sketch for the cover of *A Letter to Amy* (note the original title, *A Letter to Amelia*)

Keats posing as the model for Barney, the stepfather in *Louie's Search*

At the time of his death in 1983, Ezra Jack Keats had begun the illustrations for a Japanese folktale called "The Giant Turnip." While that book was never completed, Keats gave the world more than one hundred books featuring children from every race and ethnicity. Keats never forgot the faces and experiences of his childhood, and in his stories and art he made his neighborhood known and loved throughout the world.

Three sketches from "The Giant Turnip," the book Keats was working on at the time of his death

Observant readers should have no trouble picking him out!

No revolution is without its opposition, and for a white man creating books featuring black children, the challenges were numerous. Yet throughout all the controversy, Keats remained steadfast in his purpose: his were universal stories, depicting children who suffered hardship, found joy, and dreamed dreams. Childhood, in his mind, was a colorblind experience.

BOOKS BY EZRA JACK KEATS

My Dog Is Lost! (1960)

The Snowy Day (1962)

Whistle for Willie (1964)

Jennie's Hat (1966)

Peter's Chair (1967)

A Letter to Amy (1968)

The Little Drummer Boy (1968)

Goggles! (1969)

Hi, Cat! (1970)

Apt. 3 (1971)

Over in the Meadow (1971)

Pet Show! (1972)

Pssst! Doggie (1973)

Skates! (1973)

Dreams (1974)

Kitten for a Day (1974)

Louie (1975)

The Trip (1978)

Maggie and the Pirate (1979)

Louie's Search (1980)

Regards to the Man in the Moon (1981)

Clementina's Cactus (1982)

With special thanks to Anita Silvey, Jerry Pinkney, Simms Taback, Reynold Ruffins, Eric Carle, Martin and Lillie Pope, Deborah Pope, and Dee Jones.

VIKING
Published by the Penguin Group
Penguin Putnam Books for Young Readers,
345 Hudson Street, New York, New York 10014, U.S.A.

Penguin Books Ltd, Registered Offices: Harmondsworth, Middlesex, England

First published in 2002 by Viking, a division of Penguin Putnam Books for Young Readers.

10 9 8 7 6 5 4 3 2 1

Introduction copyright © Anita Silvey, 2002
"A Word from Jerry Pinkney" copyright © Jerry Pinkney, 2002
"A Word from Simms Taback" copyright © Simms Taback, 2002
"A Word From Eric Carle" copyright © Eric Carle, 2002
"A Word from Reynold Ruffins" copyright © Reynold Ruffins, 2002

The Snowy Day first published by The Viking Press. Copyright © Ezra Jack Keats, 1962. Copyright renewed Martin Pope, executor of the estate of Ezra Jack Keats, 1990. *Whistle for Willie* published by The Viking Press. Copyright © Ezra Jack Keats, 1964. Copyright renewed Martin Pope, 1992. *A Letter to Amy* published by Harper & Row. Copyright © Ezra Jack Keats, 1968. Copyright renewed Martin Pope, 1996. *Peter's Chair* published by Harper & Row. Copyright © Ezra Jack Keats, 1967. Copyright renewed Martin Pope, 1995. *Goggles!* published by The Macmillan Publishing Company. Copyright © Ezra Jack Keats, 1969. Copyright renewed Martin Pope, 1967. *Jennie's Hat* published by Harper & Row. Copyright © Ezra Jack Keats, 1966. Copyright renewed Martin Pope, 1994. *Hi, Cat!* published by The Macmillan Company. Copyright © Ezra Jack Keats, 1970. Copyright renewed Martin Pope, 1998. *Apt.3* published by The Macmillan Company. Copyright © Ezra Jack Keats, 1971. Copyright renewed Martin Pope, 1999. *Louie's Search* published by Four Winds Press. Copyright © Ezra Jack Keats, 1980. *Pet Show* published by The Macmillan Publishing Company. Copyright © Ezra Jack Keats, 1972. Copyright renewed Martin Pope, 2000. All rights reserved

Library of Congress Cataloging-in-Publication Data is available.

ISBN: 0-670-03586-6

Manufactured in China
Set in Bembo

Book design by Edward Miller

Illustration credits

Page 6; page 7, top left and bottom; page 9, top; page 10, top; page 121, bottom; page 122, top left, center top and bottom; page 123, top left and right; page 124, top center; page 125 and 126, all: Courtesy of the de Grummond Children's Literature Collection at the University of Southern Mississippi Libraries, Hattiesburg, Mississippi. Page 8, top left, by Ezra Jack Keats, copyright © Ezra Jack Keats Foundation, 2002; page 120 by Beverly Hall; page 121, top; page 122, bottom right; page 123, bottom: Courtesy of the Ezra Jack Keats Foundation. Page 26, top, copyright © Jerry Pinkney, 1994, from *John Henry*, by Julius Lester, illustrated by Jerry Pinkney; page 58, top, copyright © Simms Taback, 1999, from *Joseph Had a Little Overcoat* by Simms Taback; page 58, bottom, and page 101, top and bottom, copyright © 1971, Ezra Jack Keats, from *Over in the Meadow* by Ezra Jack Keats; page 89, bottom, copyright © Ezra Jack Keats, 1982, from *The King's Fountain*, by Lloyd Alexander, illustrated by Ezra Jack Keats; page 100, copyright © Eric Carle, 1981, from *The Very Hungry Caterpillar* by Eric Carle; page 124, top right, copyright © Thomas Y. Crowell Company, 1960. Copyright renewed Martin Pope, Executor of the Ezra Jack Keats Estate, 1988. From *My Dog Is Lost!* by Ezra Jack Keats and Pat Cherr: Courtesy of Penguin Putnam Inc. All rights reserved. Page 26, bottom, from *John Henry* by Ezra Jack Keats, copyright © 1965 by Ezra Jack Keats. Copyright renewed 1993 by Martin Pope, executor of the estate of the author: Used by permission of Alfred A. Knopf, an imprint of Random House Children's Books, a division of Random House, Inc. Page 124, bottom left, from *The Easter Party* (jacket cover) by Ezra Jack Keats, copyright: Used by permission of Random House Children's Books, a division of Random House, Inc. Page 88, copyright © 1996, Reynold Ruffins, from *Running the Road to ABC* by Denize Lauture, illustrated by Reynold Ruffins: Reprinted with the permission of Simon & Schuster Books for Young Readers, an imprint of Simon & Schuster Children's Publishing Division.

The
GREAT
UNSOLVED MYSTERIES
of
SCIENCE

The
GREAT
UNSOLVED MYSTERIES
of
SCIENCE

John Grant

CHARTWELL
BOOKS, INC.

A QUINTET BOOK

Published by Chartwell Books
A Division of Book Sales, Inc.
110 Enterprise Avenue
Secaucus, New Jersey 07094

ISBN 1-55521-562-9

This book was designed and produced by
Quintet Publishing Limited
6 Blundell Street
London N7 9BH

Creative Director: Peter Bridgewater
Art Director: Ian Hunt
Designer: Annie Moss
Project Editor: Caroline Beattie
Editor: Susan Baker
Picture Researcher: Liz Eddison
Illustrator: Lorraine Harrison

Typeset in Great Britain by
Central Southern Typesetters, Eastbourne
Manufactured in Hong Kong by
Regent Publishing Services Limited
Printed in Hong Kong by
Leefung-Asco Printers Limited

CONTENTS

INTRODUCTION:

Routine Magic

Arthur C Clarke once remarked that any sufficiently advanced technology is, to the rest of us, indistinguishable from magic. To see the truth of this we need only look around us. For example, I am producing these words on a word-processor which shares my life for several hours each day. I know how to make it do all kinds of things – including a few that are not in the manufacturer's manual – but I have not the first idea as to how it actually works. To me, the whole process might just as well be magic.

Science is a form of magic, too – indeed, scientists at NASA, when performing yet another theoretically impossible feat, commonly refer to it as 'routine magic'. So I make no apologies for beginning this book in the way that a conjurer might, by giving you an apparently free choice from the pack while in fact forcing on you the particular card that I want you to take.

Pick a mathematical equation – any equation. What a surprise! You happen to have chosen this one:

$$x^n + y^n = z^n$$

Now this is a very interesting equation indeed. If x, y, z and n all represent whole numbers, it appears that the equation is an impossible one for any value of n greater than 2. The word 'appears' is used advisedly because, although computers have been used to show that the equation does not work for values of n up to several thousand, no one has yet been able to prove for certain that there is *no* number n greater than 2 for which suitable values of x, y and z cannot be slotted in to produce a valid equation.

This is something of a mystery – but there is a greater mystery involved. The Frenchman Pierre de Fermat (1601–65) was one of the greatest mathematicians ever to have lived: his contributions are too many to mention. Unfortunately, he was interested in mathematics only as a hobby, and so he did not bother to publish any of his work. (It first became known to the wider world when, five years after Fermat's death, his son published his notes.)

LEFT *Home computers were unheard-of only a couple of decades ago; now they have become 'routine magic'.*

One day Fermat was reading a book on mathematics when he had an inspiration. Hastily he scribbled in the margin,

WHERE *n* IS A NUMBER LARGER THAN 2, THERE ARE NO WHOLE NUMBERS *x*, *y*, *z* SUCH THAT $x^n + y^n = z^n$, AND OF THIS I HAVE FOUND A MOST MARVELLOUS PROOF, BUT THIS MARGIN IS TOO SMALL TO CONTAIN IT.

And that is precisely *all* we have of what has now come to be known as Fermat's Last Theorem. We can discount the possibility that Fermat was lying: this was a personal note, for him alone to read. It is of course possible that he was wrong in his initial assumption – which would explain why he never expanded his 'proof' in his notes – but we have to remember that the man was a mathematical genius. For more than three centuries mathematicians have struggled to rediscover Fermat's Last Theorem, but without success. The matter is still a mystery.

Many of the mysteries of science are more important than Fermat's Last Theorem. Or are they? Even the most seemingly trivial gap in our knowledge or understanding can represent some very major failure in our comprehension – it can mean that our overall ideas are seriously wrong. This was shown dramatically in the early years of this century.

The planet Mercury orbits the Sun more closely than do any of the others. It is a small, rocky body; its surface is covered with craters and blistered by the heat of the Sun. Like the other planets it travels around the Sun in an ellipse, which means that at some times it is closer to the Sun than at others. The point of closest approach is called the *perihelion* of a planet.

All of this seemed to be well understood until early this century, because it was explained in terms of Newton's theory of gravitation. There was only one fly in the ointment – but it was the smallest, most insignificant of flies.

Mercury's perihelion *advanced* a little more than the theory said it ought to. This was discovered in about 1840 by the French astronomer Urbain Leverrier (1811–77).

When we draw a picture of a planet's orbit we show the Sun, of course, and a single line around it in the shape of an ellipse. (Imagine a 'squashed circle' with the Sun just off-

ABOVE *Pierre de Fermat, the mathematical genius who left us with one of science's greatest conundra.*

centre.) However, the truth is not quite as simple as this, because the planet does not exactly retrace its path each time it goes around the Sun. Instead, the orbit as a whole twists a little further round each time, so that a true drawing of the planet's course should really look more like one of the patterns produced by a children's Spirograph toy. The net effect is that, each time, the perihelion is a little further round than the last time – or, to put it another way, the perihelion advances. We *now* know this to be true of all the planets; however, the effect is so small that only in the case of Mercury was it detectable by nineteenth-century astronomers. And even with Mercury the change involved is minuscule: it is, in terms of angles, about 40 seconds per century (there are 3600 seconds in each degree of arc).

For several decades most scientists assumed that the discrepancy was too negligible to worry about: after all, no one said that everything in the Universe should work perfectly. Others did worry, though, and agreed with Leverrier that there must be a planet even closer to the Sun than Mercury; the gravitational tug of this hypothetical planet – which Leverrier christened Vulcan – could cause the anomalous advance of Mercury's perihelion. Astronomers made strenuous efforts to observe Vulcan, generally attributing their lack of success to the fact that a small body so close to the Sun would be incredibly difficult to detect. The whole affair seemed merely a minor mystery.

In fact it was a major mystery. Realization dawned only in 1915, when a comparatively young theoretical physicist called Albert Einstein published the paper that is now generally called the General Theory of Relativity. This theory, in passing, exactly accounted for the advance of Mercury's perihelion. More importantly, it rewrote large chunks of accepted science. Without Einstein's insight, in part inspired by the 'trivial' matter of Mercury's orbit, our knowledge of science, not to mention our technology, would be at a much lower level than it is today.

Apart from anything else, it is unlikely that anyone would have been able to develop the various forms of 'magic' that allow my word-processor to work.

This book collects together what I consider to be some of the major unsolved mysteries of science. Of course, in making my selection I am almost certainly falling into the same trap as those nineteenth-century scientists who thought that the anomalous orbit of Mercury was interesting but, in essence, a matter of little concern. At the same time, I can guarantee that some of the unsolved questions are very important indeed. There could hardly be more fundamental mysteries than the reasons why the Universe came into existence, how life began on planet Earth, and so on. Other conundra may appear rather less 'cosmically' relevant; they may seem to be of little importance yet, like Mercury's orbit, may prove in the long term to be extremely important.

Perhaps arbitrarily, this book is divided into three parts dealing, respectively, with mysteries from the past, mysteries of life, and mysteries of physics. The first section

ABOVE *Stan Gooch, the author of* Cities of Dreams.
RIGHT *Religion can be regarded as a primitive attempt to explain scientifically all the phenomena around us. This Sri Lankan Buddhist priest confronts an image of the Buddha hoping to find, through contemplation, answers to the many mysteries humanity may never find the answer to.*

essentially deals with the sciences of geology and archaeology; the second with biology, sociology, psychology and anthropology; and the third with astronomy and physics. Of course, there is no real hard-and-fast barrier between these sciences: an advance in our understanding of physics can have profound effects on our understanding of biology, and so on. This interrelation of various disciplines is fundamental to science: the word 'science' itself derives from a Latin word meaning 'knowledge' – a term that embraces far more than the circumscribed disciplines just mentioned. It seems to be part of human nature, however, to seek to categorize things, and the various aspects of what is in essence a single, broad-based quest for further knowledge and understanding have not been spared.

Here, too, we have a mystery; this time a psychological one, or perhaps it is really the province of anthropology, or archaeology, or ... Why is it that we human beings are so *curious* about everything? Why is it that we should want to know things that are, in the broad scheme, totally irrelevant? You yourself are an example of this phenomenon at work, through the simple fact that you are reading this book. Could you not equally have said: 'Ha! Mysteries of science! Leave 'em to the scientists!'